My Surprising Va...
Lewis & Clark

by Miles Parker • illustrated by John Fretz

LEWIS AND
CLARK TRAIL

Orlando   Boston   Dallas   Chicago   San Diego

Visit *The Learning Site!*

www.harcourtschool.com

Dear Maggie,

How could my parents think it would be a fun vacation to drive around the country following the path of Lewis and Clark? According to my dad, their expedition across the West in the early 1800s was a real ordeal. This trip of ours is going to be pretty dismal, too. I'll be cooped up in a car for three weeks with my brother, Tyler! What a treat!

Still, I have to admit that some of this stuff is pretty interesting. Yesterday we visited a monument in honor of Sacajawea. She was the young Native American woman who went along with her husband and baby to help guide Lewis and Clark. I guess if she could go off for three years and travel thousands of miles with her life constantly in peril, I can live through the next few weeks with Tyler.

xoxo,
Emma

Dear Maggie,

Today was kind of fun, I have to admit. We took a canoe trip on the Missouri River. It was a hot, sunny day, but the breeze off the water kept us cool. As we paddled along, I understood what Mrs. Taylor told us last year in class about rivers being the earliest kind of highway.

I know that Lewis and Clark and their group traveled by boat as much as possible on their trip. That was the easiest way for them to handle the wild terrain they had to cross.

Anyway, we're spending tonight in the Lewis and Clark Campground. You see lots of things named after the expedition out here. Yesterday, I even had a Clark Burger for lunch. It was made with buffalo meat! (It was pretty tasty, too.)

Bye for now!

xoxo,

Emma

Hi Maggie,

What a night we had! We have two tents, one for my parents and one for Tyler and me. Candy, our dog, was supposed to stay in the car, but she barked so much that Tyler and I decided she could stay in the tent with us. Big mistake!

I don't remember falling asleep, but I definitely remember waking up. Candy was barking like crazy and jumping around in the tent, which isn't all that big. Before Tyler and I could get her calmed down, she crashed into one of the walls, and the whole tent collapsed on top of us!

My parents finally got us out. We all ended up crowded into their tent. Tyler was a little scared, because he thought Candy heard a bear, but my dad says the nearest bear is about 200 miles from here.

xoxo,
Emma

Dear Maggie,

Today was really special! We went to a Native American celebration. The dancers wore gorgeous costumes and did these incredibly complicated dance steps.

Afterward, we talked to a fifteen-year-old girl who is one of the dancers. Louise (that's her name) explained the meaning of her dance. She showed us how she used dyed porcupine quills to make the designs on her costume. Louise said that dancers have always been held in special esteem by her tribe.

Louise also said that she plays basketball on her school team and wants to become a doctor, just as I do! We promised to be pen pals when I get home.

xoxo,
Emma

Hi Mags,

I'm actually having more fun than I thought I would. Even Tyler is starting to seem OK.

The other day we visited the Great Falls of the Missouri River. They are really an impressive sight, with tons of water roaring over a huge drop.

I can only imagine how discouraging it must have been when the Lewis and Clark group first saw those falls. To get past them, the group had to push, pull, and carry their boats and supplies up and around the falls. It took them twenty-four days!

We're in Montana now. This is real cowboy country. Needless to say, Tyler is excited. When he saw a sign for a rodeo, he talked Mom and Dad into making a detour.

I thought it would be pretty boring, but it turned out to be great. I especially liked the clowns. They're dressed like the ones in the circus, but they actually have an important job. When one of the rodeo riders gets thrown off a horse or a bull, the clowns make sure the animal doesn't step on the rider.

Tyler and I met a couple of local kids at the rodeo. They were entered in the junior events. Danny came in second in calf roping and first in calf riding. His sister, Julie, finished third in the riding event.

Afterward, Danny and Julie's parents invited us all to spend the night at their ranch. I thought Tyler was going to float off the ground! We had a great time. When we got up the next day, we all went for a horseback ride. Tyler has already decided that he's going to live out here when he grows up. We invited Danny and Julie to visit us next summer. They've never been to a really big city. I guess what you already have always seems less exciting than what you don't have. Do you know what I mean?

xoxo,
Emma

Hi Mags,

We're heading home, in a roundabout way. Instead of continuing west to the Pacific, as Lewis and Clark did, we're curving around in a big circle.

We're spending a few days in Yellowstone National Park. Yesterday we went for a nature hike led by one of the park rangers. He told us what to do in case we should see a grizzly bear. Then he said a large group like ours would scare most bears away. That sounds just fine to me!

Anyway, we didn't see any bears, but we did see some deer and a pair of bald eagles sitting in a tree. The eagles were so close you could see the yellow in their eyes. They were beautiful in a fierce kind of way. I doubt I'll ever see a bald eagle at our backyard bird feeder!

xoxo,
Emma

Hi Maggie,

Wow! What a day this has been! Mom and I went white-water rafting. (Tyler was too young to go, so Dad stayed with him.) There were ten people in the raft, in addition to the guide. On some rafts the passengers just go along for the ride, but we actually paddled.

It was unbelievable! You could say it was like a water-park ride, only a hundred times better! Every time we hit a stretch of really wild water, the guide told us what to do. Then, all of a sudden, water was crashing into us, and we were bouncing around like a toy boat. We got completely soaked! Everybody was yelling and laughing at once. We covered 8 miles of river. By the time we were done, my knees felt like jelly.

No matter what Candy does tonight, I won't have any trouble sleeping. See you soon.

xoxo,
Emma

Hi Maggie,

   Candy got herself into trouble yesterday. There are strict rules in Yellowstone about keeping dogs leashed, so that they won't chase any of the wildlife. Tyler <u>had</u> Candy on a leash while we were all walking on a trail. All of a sudden, a rabbit darted in front of us. Candy yanked so hard on the leash that Tyler let go. She took off into the woods so fast that we never had a chance to stop her. We called her name, but she didn't come back.

   Tyler was pretty upset, and, to tell the truth, I was kind of scared, too. I mean, what if Candy ran into a bear or something?

So, we went back to our camp and told a ranger what had happened. I don't know whether Tyler was more afraid of getting into trouble or of what might happen to Candy in the woods.

Anyway, the ranger said he'd alert the other campsites and rangers. He said Candy would probably get picked up by somebody. I guess he was trying to make us feel better, but I could tell from Tyler's face that it wasn't working.

I was really nervous, especially when six hours went by. Then, just before dark, the ranger walked up to our tent, leading Candy by her leash. He said she'd been found by a group of hikers. We thanked him profusely, with all of us hugging Candy at the same time. I was so relieved and happy that I didn't know whether to laugh or cry.

xoxo,
Emma

Dear Maggie,

We are definitely on our way home! Yesterday, we left Yellowstone, and now we're heading east across Montana. This is the route Lewis and Clark followed on their way home, too. Once they actually reached the Pacific, in November 1805, they still had to get back. The plan was to hitch a ride from a ship's captain and sail home by going all the way around the tip of South America. When no ship had shown up by March 1806, the group just packed up and started back by land.

I wonder whether going back seemed easier or harder to them. What do you think?

See you SOON!

Emma

MONTANA

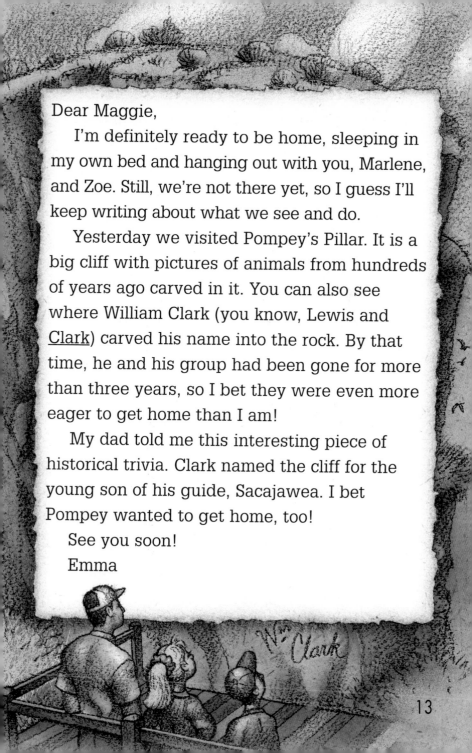

Dear Maggie,

I'm definitely ready to be home, sleeping in my own bed and hanging out with you, Marlene, and Zoe. Still, we're not there yet, so I guess I'll keep writing about what we see and do.

Yesterday we visited Pompey's Pillar. It is a big cliff with pictures of animals from hundreds of years ago carved in it. You can also see where William Clark (you know, Lewis and <u>Clark</u>) carved his name into the rock. By that time, he and his group had been gone for more than three years, so I bet they were even more eager to get home than I am!

My dad told me this interesting piece of historical trivia. Clark named the cliff for the young son of his guide, Sacajawea. I bet Pompey wanted to get home, too!

See you soon!

Emma

Hi Mags,

We stopped yesterday to visit a place called the Spirit Mound. It's a hill that Native American tribes once believed to be inhabited by 18-inch-high spirits. It took Lewis and Clark four hours to walk to the hill after they spotted it. It took us just a few minutes to get there by car. If you ask permission, which we did, you can walk to the top.

In his journal, William Clark reported that from the top of the Spirit Mound, he and his companions could see "numerous herds of buffalo feeding in various directions." We saw mostly cars on Highway 19. Come to think of it, from far enough away, they did look sort of like a herd of animals moving along together.

I'll be home soon!

xoxo,

Emma

Hi Maggie,

Today my dad wanted to visit the Lewis and Clark State Park, where there are replicas of the different kinds of boats Lewis and Clark used on their expedition.

As we were packing up our camping gear, Mom said, "Emma, what do you say you and I just do something a little different?" So we dropped my dad and Tyler off and took the car into town.

Mom and I had lunch and just hung around. (I had my last buffalo burger for a while!) It felt as if we were back home, even though we're not actually there yet. Do you think that's weird?

Your buddy,
Emma

Hi Maggie,

 By the time you get this, I'll already be home. I just wanted to write one last time, because writing to you has been a big part of this trip.

 When we set out on this trip, I didn't think it would be much fun. However, I have to admit that I was wrong. We saw so many amazing places and did so many unforgettable things. Besides, I got a sense of just how big this country is and how big it must have seemed before people could fly or drive across it. Best of all, I got to know my little brother better. He even turned out to be a great, back-seat game player.

 Your best friend forever,
 Emma

Chicago
200 miles